Ready for wings

"Oh, I'm so excited. I have all my feathers except for one small patch. This job will fill it in and I'll earn my wings, I just know I will." The Little Angel of Fairness took the archangel's hand and held it tightly. "Where are we going?"

"To a driveway in front of a garage."

What kind of bells are in a garage, wondered the little angel; for every time angels earn their wings, a bell will ring. What kind of bell would ring when she earned her wings?

Sheard

Aladdin
Angelwings
No. 6

No Fair!

Donna Jo Napoli
illustrations by Lauren Klementz-Harte

Aladdin Paperbacks
New York   London   Toronto   Sydney   Singapore

Thank you to all my family,
Brenda Bowen, Nöelle Paffett-Lugassy, and Richard Tchen

First Aladdin Paperbacks edition February 2000

Text copyright © 2000 by Donna Jo Napoli
Illustrations copyright © 2000 by Lauren Klementz-Harte

Aladdin Paperbacks
An imprint of Simon & Schuster
Children's Publishing Division
1230 Avenue of the Americas
New York, NY 10020

Designed by Steve Scott
The text for this book was set in Minister Light and Cheltenham.
Printed and bound in the United States of America
10 9 8 7 6 5 4 3 2 1

Library of Congress Cataloging-in-Publication Data
Napoli, Donna Jo, 1948–
No fair! / Donna Jo Napoli ; illustrations by Lauren Klementz-Harte.
p.   cm. — (Aladdin Angelwings ; #6)
Summary: To earn her wings, the Little Angel of Fairness tries to help
Jessica get her brother Hank to allow her to be in the town parade with
him, even though she is a girl.
ISBN 0-689-83206-0 (pbk.)
[1. Angels—Fiction. 2. Brothers and sisters—Fiction.
3. Sex roles—Fiction.]
I. Klementz-Harte, Lauren, 1961– ill. II. Title. III. Series: Napoli,
Donna Jo, 1948–   Aladdin angelwings ; #6.
PZ7.N15No   2000
99-38627
CIP

*To Barry,
who knew from
the beginning*

Angel Talk

"One for you and one for me, and one for you and one for me." The Little Angel of Fairness counted out chocolate Kisses. Chocolate was her favorite, and Kisses were the best. There was one left over.

"I get it," said the Little Angel of Friendship.

The Little Angel of Fairness pushed her glasses up her nose and neatly arranged her pile of chocolate Kisses into a pyramid. "We have to share it."

"It's too small to share. Plus, if you give it to me, then you'll feel terrific for being generous and I can feel terrific for giving you the opportunity to be so generous."

The Little Angel of Fairness laughed. She unwrapped the tinfoil from the candy Kiss and took out a pair of tiny scissors. "I'll cut it in half, and you can choose the half you want."

"You're going to cut it with scissors?"

"That's all I have. Aren't they cute?" The Little Angel of Fairness cut carefully, but one piece of the Kiss was slightly bigger than the other, anyway.

The Little Angel of Friendship put his hand out toward the big piece. Then he grinned and popped the smaller piece in his mouth.

"Well done," said the Archangel of Fairness. "You're both acting like perfect angels this morning."

"What else would you expect?" said the Little Angel of Friendship.

"Perhaps a bit of humility." The Archangel of Fairness raised her eyebrows in a look of mock scolding. Then she smiled. "Put away your chocolate for now, my little angel, and say good-bye to your buddy." She leaned over the Little Angel of Fairness. "You have a job to do."

"Yay!" The Little Angel of Fairness kissed

the other little angel on the cheek. "When I get back, we can play a spinning game with the gold coins I've been collecting."

"But I was supposed to choose our next game," said the Little Angel of Friendship.

"You'll like this game."

"You always choose," said the Little Angel of Friendship. "And I'm always forced to go along."

"So what? You always have fun. My games are the best." The Little Angel of Fairness stuffed her chocolate Kisses into her right pocket. "Oh, I'm so excited. I have all my feathers except for one small patch. This job will fill it in, and I'll earn my wings, I just know I will."

"Good luck," called the Little Angel of Friendship.

The Little Angel of Fairness waved goodbye. Then she took the archangel's hand and held it tightly. "Where are we going?"

"To a driveway in front of a garage."

What kinds of bells are in a garage? wondered the little angel; for every time angels earn their wings, a bell will ring. What kind of bell would ring when she earned her wings?

She put her hand in her left pocket—the one where she kept her gold coins—and she clinked them together softly. They sounded almost like a small, tinkling bell.

Bikes

Hank loosened the nut with a wrench. Then he jiggled his bicycle seat and pulled upward until it was an inch higher. "Just right," he said softly. He opened the pack of spaceship decals he'd bought at the pharmacy and pressed one onto his right handlebar. It shone silvery and perfect.

"Your decals are pretty," said Jessica, coming up behind him. She had a book tucked under one arm. "Will you fix my seat now? It needs to be raised, too. I'm growing as fast as you are."

"You'll never be as tall as me." Hank looked at Jessica's bike, leaning against the side of the garage. "There's a cobweb in your spokes. When's the last time you rode that thing?"

"I forget."

"I'm not going to waste my time working on your bike if you aren't even going to ride it."

"I'll ride it," said Jessica.

"Where?"

"Where are you going to ride yours?" asked Jessica.

"In the high school's Homecoming parade on Saturday afternoon. All my friends are going to be in it."

"I'll ride in the parade, too."

"No way," said Hank. "The bike part of the parade is only for guys."

"That's not fair."

"Come on, Jessica, you can't butt in on a guy thing."

"I can do anything you can."

"Then fix your own seat."

"I'm not strong enough, and you know it." Jessica wrinkled her nose at Hank. "Can I at least have some decals to decorate my bike?"

Hank clutched his decals to his chest. "I paid for these with my own money."

"I don't have any money," said Jessica.

"So what? I paid, and these decals are mine."

"Remember when you needed sequins for your school project? I let you take a bunch off my dancing costume."

Hank swung one leg over and perched on his bike seat. His feet just reached the ground. "You hated your dancing costume. You hate dancing." He rolled forward. This height for the seat felt good.

"So what?" said Jessica. She took a step and planted herself right in his path. "I shared with you."

"It's not the same thing. Besides, these are spaceships. See?" Hank flashed the decals in front of Jessica's face, then jammed them in his pocket. "They don't go on a girl's bike."

"Oh, yeah? Well, I don't really want them, anyway," said Jessica. "Spaceships have nothing to do with real ships."

"What are you talking about?" asked Hank.

"The theme for Homecoming is always pirates. The high school football team is the Pirates. You know that."

"Of course I know that. But I don't care," said Hank. "Just because the team is the Pirates doesn't mean I have to like pirates. But I do like spaceships. And you can't have any of my decals."

"You stink," said Jessica.

"Go read your dumb book," said Hank.

"It's not dumb." Jessica patted her book. "You haven't read it. You never read. I read all the time and I'm a year and a half younger than you. Besides, I just finished my book."

"Then go read another one," said Hank.

"I will. I'll know everything, and you'll know nothing," said Jessica. "And that's how it should be, 'cause you stink."

Angel Talk

"H e does stink," said the Little Angel of Fairness.

"All right, then," said the Archangel of Fairness. "Help him learn."

The little angel stuck a chocolate Kiss in her mouth. She held one up to the archangel. "Want one?"

"Thanks." The Archangel of Fairness unwrapped the candy.

The little angel smiled. "I know: I'll take half of his money and give it to his sister."

The archangel looked surprised. "So you think money is his problem?"

"Don't you?" asked the little angel.

"No." She ate her chocolate and licked her fingers. "Besides, if you give Hank's money to Jessica, that won't teach him anything about fairness."

"All right, then, I'll find a way to make him share his money with her so she can buy decals, too."

"That's a little better," said the Archangel of Fairness, "although I don't really like putting so much importance on the money side of things. And, anyway, little angel, he might have spent all of his money already."

"Well, I can fix that," said the little angel. "Oh, yes, I can fix that with something that will be just perfect."

Gold

Hank put his favorite bowl on the table and set his favorite spoon beside it. Then he looked through the set of twelve miniature boxes of sugar cereals.

"I get the marshmallow ones," said Jessica. She ripped open the cellophane and grabbed a box. "Mom must really be afraid of her test next week to buy such great junk food."

"It's important. Her midterm, or something like that. I can't wait till she finishes this stupid computer course."

Jessica dumped cereal in her bowl. She picked out a tiny marshmallow and popped it in her mouth. "Yum. I wish she'd buy this kind of cereal all the time. Taste this." She handed Hank a marshmallow.

ﾊy. It
gave an
ﾞ up the box
ﾚhe back. "This
ﾙe first ingredient is

ﾗgar's the second ingredient.
ﾚ, anyway. I like sugar."
ﾚank. He chose a box with pictures
of fruit all over it and poured. Many-colored,
doughnut-shaped rings filled his bowl.

Clunk!

"What was that?" asked Jessica.

"Look." Hank held up a gold coin.

Jessica turned her empty cereal box
upside down and shook hard. "No fair."

"That's life." Hank slipped the coin into his
pocket. Its weight felt comfortably important.

"Let me see it," said Jessica.

"Later, maybe. If I feel like it."

"What are you going to do with it?" asked
Jessica.

"I haven't decided yet. Maybe I could get a million pairs of new sneakers."

"You can't get sneakers with pretend money. Let's play pirates," said Jessica.

"How do you know it's pretend?"

"Give me a break."

Hank put his hand in his pocket and felt the coin. It was real metal, at least. And it was so heavy. "You can't be a pirate, anyway."

"Sure I can."

"No you can't. There were no girl pirates."

Jessica wrinkled her nose at Hank. "There had to be girl pirates. There are girl everythings, it's just that most people don't know it. Plus I'd make a better pirate than you any day."

"Well, too bad," Hank said, gobbling his cereal. "I got the gold coin, and you didn't."

"Doubloon," said Jessica.

"Mom!" screamed Hank. "Jessica just cursed at me."

"That's nice, honey," called Mom from her study.

"Taking that class is turning Mom into a lunatic," said Hank.

"You're the lunatic," said Jessica. "'Doubloon' isn't a curse word. It's what pirates called gold coins."

Hank finished his cereal and drank the milk from the bottom of the bowl. "How do you know?"

"Hank, if you'd only read now and then, you'd know things, too. The newspaper has an article about doubloons, because of Homecoming. There's going to be a fair all weekend, and this year everyone's going to be paying for everything with doubloons."

"Where are people going to get doubloons from?" asked Hank.

Jessica screwed up her face. "I don't know. I didn't finish the article." She looked through the newspaper.

Hank grabbed the paper from her and read. "The high school is selling them. It's sort of like buying tickets for the rides at the state fair."

"Maybe they're giving them away in cereal boxes, too," said Jessica. "Maybe that's why you got one now."

"I don't think so," Hank said, quickly putting his hand in his pocket. Yes, the coin was heavy and too hard to bend. "Mine is special."

"Hey," said Jessica, "we can buy a whole bunch of Homecoming doubloons and play pirates all the time."

"Not with my money. I think I'll just hang on to this special gold coin—this special *doubloon*," said Hank, emphasizing the last word. "And if you don't eat fast, you're going to miss the school bus."

Angel Talk

"Exactly how is that gold coin helping?" asked the Archangel of Fairness.

"I'm not sure yet, but it is money, at least." The Little Angel of Fairness smiled. "I think I'll get Hank to buy something nice that he can share with Jessica. She has a sweet tooth, just like me. Maybe I'll get him to buy a lot of chocolate Kisses."

The Archangel of Fairness looked off to the side.

The little angel followed her gaze. There was nothing there. She knew from past experience that when the archangel looked off at nothing, that meant the archangel wanted her to think harder. "Or maybe I'll have him sell it to a bank for regular money that he can divide fairly with her."

The Archangel of Fairness tapped her foot and hummed to herself.

"Or . . . ," said the little angel slowly, hoping another, better, idea would come to her. She unwrapped two chocolate Kisses. "Want one?"

"No thanks. I've eaten too many sweets lately." The archangel looked down and appeared to be checking her slippers.

The little angel put both Kisses in her mouth. "I've got it," she said.

"What?" asked the archangel.

"You'll see."

More Gold

The next morning Jessica was already eating when Hank came down to breakfast. Jessica was surrounded by miniature cereal boxes— all open. She looked at Hank and stuck out her tongue.

Hank smiled and reached for one of the regular-sized boxes of cereal. "Looks like I got the only doubloon." He poured a bowl of Wheat Chex.

Clunk!

Hank searched through the cereal with his fingers. "Another one."

"Ahhhh!" screamed Jessica. She beat her fists on the table. "Ahhhh!"

"Stop acting like a baby," said Hank. He ate his cereal while turning over the new doubloon in his other hand. This really was

remarkable: two doubloons, and they weren't even in the same kind of cereal box. "Boy, am I lucky."

"You have to share now. You've got two."

"Nu-uh. If you'd been meant to have a doubloon, one would have come out of your cereal box. These were meant for me."

"I'll tell Mom," said Jessica.

"We're not supposed to bother Mom while she's studying, and you know it."

"This is so unfair," whined Jessica. "You don't even know what to do with doubloons."

"I've been thinking about it," said Hank. And he had, ever since he'd put his shorts on this morning and felt that weight in his pocket again. "I might get a Ferrari."

"What's that?"

"The best car in the world. They start at sixty thousand dollars. Or maybe seventy. Any guy knows that."

"You can't even drive. And you can't buy anything with pretend doubloons, anyway,

Hank. Anybody with a brain knows that."

Hank almost said the coins were real, but he caught himself in time. They looked real; they felt real. But real gold doesn't come out of cereal boxes. He put the doubloon in his pocket. It made a nice *clink* against the other one.

"Come on, Hank. Forget about buying sneakers and crazy cars. If you were really meant to have these doubloons, you were meant to play pirates with them. So play with me when we get home from school today." Jessica got on her knees on her chair and leaned out halfway across the breakfast table till her face was close to Hank's. "Come on, Hankie. Please."

"I hate it when you call me Hankie. Pirates don't say things like that. That's girl talk."

"I can talk like a pirate if I want, you scurvy swashbuckler. And there were at least two famous girl pirates: Mary and Anne."

"You made that up. Those are the most common names in the world."

"So what? They're real. They were both on the fiercest pirate ship. A warship was sent to capture the pirates, and at the end of the sword fight, Mary and Anne were the last two pirates left standing."

"That's probably because no one wanted to kill a woman."

"They were dressed as men. No one knew they were women. And Anne was a better sword fighter than any of the men. So there," said Jessica. "I read about them last night, Mr. Stinky. I got a whole book on pirates from the school library yesterday."

"Why?"

"Well, 'cause of the Homecoming parade and everything."

Hank finished his bowl of cereal. "Well, after school today you can just keep reading. That's what girls do. And I'll keep counting my money. That's what guys do."

Angel Talk

Two coins don't seem any better than one," said the archangel.

"That's because he's even more stingy than I thought. He was supposed to give one to her." The Little Angel of Fairness took out a chocolate and let it melt slowly in her mouth. "I don't understand why he's so unfair with money."

"You're on the wrong track, little angel."

"What do you mean?"

"I said it before: Money isn't the true problem," said the Archangel of Fairness. "Think about it. If you were Hank, what would you be doing now?"

"Playing pirates with Jessica."

"Exactly. But Hank won't."

The little angel nodded. "Because he thinks

girls can't be pirates. And, oh, he thought girls couldn't have spaceship decals. And he doesn't want a girl to ride in the parade. He's got the wrong idea about girls."

"Bingo," said the archangel.

"Oh," said the little angel. "All along I've been trying to find ways to get him to share the gold coins with her—half and half, like I always share with my friends. But not giving people a chance is just as bad as not sharing."

"There are lots of ways to be unfair," said the archangel.

"And this way is driving Jessica crazy."

"So, now that you know the real problem," said the archangel, "what are you going to do about it?"

More and More Gold

The kitchen was empty when Hank came down to breakfast. He picked up the box of Cheerios.

"Mine!" shouted Jessica, jumping out from under the table. She grabbed the box and ripped it open. Cheerios flew everywhere.

Hank looked from the mess on the floor to the thin patch of black cloth on the counter. "Is that yours?"

Jessica squashed the empty Cheerios box with both hands and stamped through the pile of oats. "I want a doubloon. I want a doubloon. I want a doubloon."

"You'd better clean that up before Mom comes down." Hank picked up the black cloth. It had a piece of string attached to it. "What is this?"

Jessica snatched it and tied the string around her head so that the patch covered one eye. She glowered at Hank with the other eye. "Eyes go fast in sword fights," she said threateningly.

"Only if you're a poor fencer," said Hank. "I've never lost an eye."

"You've never been in a sword fight."

"Neither have you," said Hank.

"Shows how much you know," said Jessica. She straightened her eye patch and took out the broom and dustpan.

"Where'd you get that eye patch, anyway?"

"Play pirates with me and I'll make one for you."

"With a girl? Never." Hank picked up the box of Raisin Bran and poured a bowl.

Clunk! Clunk!

"Two!" Jessica threw herself on the floor. "No, no, no!" She rolled in the Cheerios dust.

Hank was almost dizzy with amazement. What on earth was going on? He must be the richest kid in the world. He dropped both coins in his pocket with the others. He would jingle-jangle his way through the day. "Should I buy the city zoo and set all the animals free?"

"You're an animal," said Jessica.

"Should I go on TV and run for president?"

"Run for idiot is more like it," said Jessica.

"Should I—"

"Shut up! We should play pirates after school today, Mr. Stinky Stinky Stinky." Jessica scooped up two handfuls of smashed Cheerios and dumped them on Hank's head.

Angel Talk

$\mathscr{J}$ thought we agreed money wasn't the issue," said the Archangel of Fairness.

"We did. But money is a tool in my plan." The little angel unwrapped a chocolate Kiss, threw it in the air, and caught it in her mouth. "Want to try?"

"Sure." The archangel unwrapped the Kiss the little angel gave her and threw it in the air. It came down smack on her nose and fell to the ground.

"It takes a little practice. Here, try again."

"No thanks. Let's pay attention to our problem. You have to do more than fill Hank's pockets with coins."

"I am doing more," said the little angel. "Who do you think found that patch of black cloth in the sewing basket and put it on the floor of Jessica's closet? She's so smart—she knew instantly that it would make a perfect eye patch. And wait'll you see what else I put there."

"What?"

The little angel laughed.

Pirates' Garb

On Saturday morning when Hank walked into the kitchen, Jessica was standing in front of the cereal cupboard, one eye covered by the patch and a rubber sword in her hands. "Which box? Tell me or die!"

"I'm having eggs," said Hank.

Jessica pulled at her hair and ran screaming into the living room.

Hank followed her. "Where'd you get that sword?"

"It's called a 'rapier,' actually. And pirates don't tell landlubbers." Jessica stuck her hand deep in her jeans pocket and pulled out a bandanna. She tied it around her head.

Hank walked in a circle around Jessica. "With that bandanna on, your hair doesn't even show. You could be a boy pirate."

"I'm a girl pirate," shouted Jessica. She pointed her rapier at him. "And you're a boy ape."

"Have you got any more of those rapiers?"

"No," said Jessica. "But I've got a toy cutlass."

"What's that?" asked Hank.

"It's like a sword, but the blade is shorter."

"Oh," Hank said, looking wistfully at the rapier.

"But the cutlass blade is also a lot broader. It can hack people apart," said Jessica.

"Really?" Hank scratched his head. "Well, maybe I'll play with you, but I'm having breakfast first." He marched into the kitchen and put a frying pan on the stove.

"What are you doing?"

"Watch." Hank let a pat of butter melt in the middle of the pan, then he cracked an egg into it.

"How'd you learn how to cook an egg?"

"Mom taught me last night, when you were

off reading. I made one for her during her study break. With toast. And a glass of milk."

Jessica grabbed a fork and poked the yolk. Yellow ran everywhere.

"Hey, what's the big idea?" said Hank.

"Just checking," said Jessica. "That yolk looked a lot like gold."

Hank burst out laughing. "All right, if you want to play pirates so bad, I'll play with you."

"Yay!" Jessica yelled up the stairs, "Bye, Mom, we're going sailing."

"That's nice, honey," called Mom from her study.

"What do you mean, we're going sailing?" asked Hank. "We can't go sailing."

"Yes we can," said Jessica. "Mom said so."

"Her test is Monday," said Hank, gobbling up the egg. "She's totally loopy. She didn't understand a word you said."

"That's her fault, not mine," said Jessica. "Let's get our bikes."

"Where can we go sailing, anyway?"

"Moon Bay."

Hank stuffed the last bite of toast into his mouth. "I've never heard of Moon Bay."

"That's because it's a pirate secret," said Jessica. She went to her room and came out wearing a backpack and holding her toy rapier in one hand and the cutlass in the other. She handed the cutlass to Hank as they went outside.

"We can't ride bikes with swords in our hands," said Hank.

"That's what the straps are for. They can hang across our backs." Jessica climbed on her bike and led the way down the sidewalk. She turned right onto Forest Drive. Then she stopped.

"This is the soccer field," said Hank.

"That's one of its many disguises," said Jessica. "It's really a big bay. Moon Bay."

"You're nuts," said Hank. "I knew we weren't really going sailing."

Jessica pulled her rapier out of the

36

scabbard and cut a figure eight high in the air. Then she put it on the ground and opened up her backpack. She took out a purple bedsheet with two holes cut in it. "Here. You step in one hole and I'll step in the other, and we can drape the sheet over both our bikes and ride along under it."

"Why?" asked Hank.

"Just do it."

"I have to be back in time to ride my bike in the parade this afternoon," said Hank.

"It's only ten. And the parade doesn't start till after lunch."

"But I have to get ready for it," said Hank.

"You are ready," said Jessica. "You already put decals on your bike. Let's play."

Angel Talk

Swords?" The Archangel of Fairness moaned softly. "Oh, no."

"They're not real," said the little angel. "They're rubber. But they look good, don't they?"

"Oh, rubber. That's good. But the sheet is real."

"A sheet's not dangerous," said the Little Angel of Fairness.

"Maybe not, but what do you think that mother's going to say when Jessica tells her she cut two big holes in her sheet?"

"'That's nice, honey,'" called the little angel, mimicking the mother perfectly.

The archangel laughed. "Well, I don't know exactly what you're up to, and I have no idea what Jessica's up to with that sheet, but you've got Hank agreeing to play pirates with Jessica, and that's a start. So keep at it."

Moon Bay

"Watch out for alligators," said Jessica.

"Alligators?" said Hank. "There are no alligators in the high seas." Jessica said stupid things, but they were spooky and they made him feel odd. He found himself looking around carefully in spite of himself.

"Lots of pirates hid in the bayous of Louisiana, and the waters there are croc-infested."

"'Croc-infested'? Listen to the way you talk. You sound like a book."

"I sound like a pirate."

"I thought this was a bay," said Hank. "Not a bayou."

"Oh, yeah, I forgot," said Jessica. She pointed over at the edge of the field. "Look at

all those schooners. Let's attack them. Charge!" she shouted.

"Schooners?" asked Hank. "I don't see anything."

"Those big boats." Jessica leaned close and whispered, "The imaginary ones. We're in a schooner, too. Just a small one. Pirates had little schooners so they could go fast."

"This is a schooner?"

"Yeah, pedal."

Hank and Jessica pedaled. The sheet got caught in the front wheel. They jerked to a stop.

"This isn't working," said Hank.

"It will," said Jessica. "We just need to find a way to keep the sheet off the wheel."

"That's not all," said Hank. "This doesn't look one bit like a schooner."

"Sure it does."

"No it doesn't. It looks like an ugly old purple sheet over two bikes."

"Mom always says you can't criticize unless you have a better idea," said Jessica.

"Moon Bay is yucky," said Hank. "I'm going home." He stepped out of the sheet and pulled his bike free.

Angel Talk

Well, that certainly didn't last long," said the Archangel of Fairness. "Hank's on his way home."

"He doesn't give Jessica half a chance," said the little angel. "I don't know what to do about him. Hey, what would you think if I put a bunch of chocolate Kisses in Jessica's pocket? Then she could lure Hank into playing by feeding them to him, one for each nice thing he did."

"That sounds like bribery to me," said the archangel. "And bribery doesn't teach anyone anything. Besides, you already pointed out that she's the one with the sweet tooth, not Hank."

"Well, then, I'm just going to have to get him to see what fun it would be to play pirates with her."

"How?" asked the archangel.

"I don't know. But Hank is still driving Jessica nuts, and now he's driving me nuts, too. This calls for drastic action, and I'm ready."

The Schooner

Hank rode his bike in the middle of the street. Jessica was far behind him, riding on the sidewalk, because Mom didn't allow her to ride in the street.

There was a trash pile up ahead on the right. Someone had put out a huge cardboard box, big enough for a refrigerator to come in. All of a sudden the box seemed to move on its own. It tumbled out into the street, right into Hank's path.

Crash.

Hank laid on the ground. Little stars spun in circles before his eyes.

"Oh, Hank, are you okay?" Jessica leaned over him. She looked like she was about to cry. "Get up out of the street, fast." She pulled on his hand.

45

Hank stood up and rubbed his left arm. It was bruised. But besides that, he felt fine. "That giant box fell in my way."

"I know. I saw what happened. You couldn't help it." Jessica brushed at Hank's shirt. "Are you hurt?"

Hank shook his head. He looked at Jessica's anxious face. Then he looked at the box again. "Do you think you could walk both our bikes home?"

"If you feel that bad, sure," said Jessica. "We've only got a block to go."

"I don't feel bad. I've got an idea." Hank dragged the box along the sidewalk while Jessica walked both bikes behind him. He went straight to the garage. "Let's let Mom know we're back, in case she worried."

They opened the house door.

Jessica stuck her head inside. "Hi, Mom, we're home."

"We almost drowned at sea," Hank called past her shoulder.

"That's nice, honey," called Mom from her study.

Hank and Jessica looked at each other and smiled.

Hank shut the door and led the way into the garage. "Give me your sheet."

Jessica looked at Hank wide-eyed. Then she ripped open her backpack and handed Hank the sheet.

Hank laid the box on its side. "See how it's shaped sort of like a boat? Help me."

Together they spread the sheet over the box.

"Our own schooner," said Jessica proudly.

"Now all we have to do is cut the other side out of the box, so our bikes can go under it."

"And we need two holes in the top, so the top halves of our bodies can stick out," said Jessica.

"And holes for our hands, to steer the bikes," said Hank.

They worked side by side, Jessica drawing

47

where the cuts should go, and Hank working with the scissors. They put the box over the bikes and put the sheet over everything. Then they crawled underneath and came up through the two holes, sitting on the bike seats.

"Ready?" said Hank. "One two three."

They pedaled.

Jessica wobbled to one side. "I'm not strong enough to pedal with all this extra weight."

"Hmm. Well, I guess we can just straddle our bikes and walk them."

They walked out to the sidewalk.

"This is easy," said Jessica. "We're pirates."

"It still doesn't look like a schooner," said Hank. "We need a mast."

"Pirate schooners had two masts," said Jessica.

Hank thought about that. He grinned. "Wait." He put down his kickstand. Then he climbed out from under the boat and ran into the garage. A few minutes later he came back with two push brooms and a wrench. "Here, unscrew these broom poles."

Jessica unscrewed the poles from the broom bottoms.

Hank used the wrench to take the seat off his bike. Then he took the seat off Jessica's bike. He smiled at her and jammed a broom pole into the tube that his bike seat came out of.

"Oh, you're so smart." Jessica jammed the other broom pole into the tube for her bike seat.

"Now we need sails," said Hank.

"Pillowcases would do great," said Jessica.

"And we need to look right," said Hank. "You've got a bandanna and a patch, but I don't have anything."

"I can make you a scarf out of my old pajamas," said Jessica. "And we can put on white shirts. Pirates liked white shirts."

Hank didn't know what he thought of tying Jessica's old pajamas around his head, but that wasn't the most pressing problem right now. "We need a black flag with a skull and crossbones."

"The costume store in town has everything," said Jessica. "Let's go shopping." She put down her kickstand and crawled out from under the boat.

Hank looked admiringly at the two masts. Then he frowned. "Who's supposed to pay for a flag?"

"We've got doubloons," said Jessica.

"Not '*we,*'" Hank said, "*me.*"

"What good's money if you don't know how to spend it?" said Jessica.

Hank put his hand in his pocket and made a fist around the coins. It had been fun having these jangling around the past few days. And it had been extra fun knowing how much Jessica wished she'd gotten them in her cereal, too. But dressing the bikes up like a pirate ship was even more fun. "All right."

Angel Talk

That was the most irresponsible thing I ever saw a little angel do," said the Archangel of Fairness. "How could you!"

The little angel folded her hands together tight. "What are you talking about?"

"You pushed that box in front of Hank's bike, didn't you?"

"Yes," said the little angel.

"What were you thinking of? Hank could have been truly hurt."

"But he wasn't," said the little angel. "He even said he didn't feel bad."

"That's not the point. What if he had hit his head hard on the pavement? What if a car had come along when he was lying there?"

"Oh," said the Little Angel of Fairness. "Oh, no. You're right." Her face crumpled, and

a tear rolled down her cheek. "I'm so sorry. The box was just lying there and it seemed like such a perfect boat. And I was so frustrated with Hank because nothing seemed to work with him. So I pushed the box without really thinking the whole thing through. I'm sorry."

"Promise me you'll think things through from now on."

"I promise," said the little angel, swallowing her sobs.

"Well, all right, then." The archangel sat down and pulled the little angel onto her lap. "Don't cry. You've got Hank completely involved in playing pirates now. So at least something good came of it."

The little angel sniffed and wiped her cheeks. "But the most important problem hasn't been solved yet."

"You've got time," said the archangel. "You'll do it. I have faith in you."

The Costume Store

The three-cornered hat sat on the shelf. Hank stared at it.

Jessica came up behind him. "That would make you look like a pirate captain for real. You'd better buy it."

Hank picked up the hat and looked at the price tag. "Everything in this costume store costs too much."

Jessica stroked the stuffed parrot on her shoulder. "We've got four doubloons. We can afford it."

"How do you know? The price is in dollars, not doubloons."

"I just know," said Jessica. "And look." She pointed at a big white shirt at the front of a rack. "You should wear that."

"But it has lace at the wrists."

"And at the throat, too. It's a pirate captain's shirt," said Jessica. "Put it on."

Hank put the big shirt on over his own. He tightened the lace at the wrists to keep the sleeves from covering his hands. Neatened up like that, the shirt did carry a sense of authority. He puffed out his chest.

"That looks nice, Hank." Jessica put the three-cornered hat on his head. "We're a scary pair. Oh, look." Jessica ran over to an open treasure box, full of costume jewelry. She held up a string of pearls. "Wouldn't this look great on me?"

Hank fingered the coins in his pocket. They had already chosen a big black pirate flag and the parrot on Jessica's shoulder. Now he wanted both the shirt and the hat. There would never be enough money for pearls, too. "I thought you said girl pirates dressed like boys."

Jessica looked at Hank and blinked. Then

she put the pearls back in the box. "We'd better pay and go."

"Don't act like that," said Hank.

"Like what?" said Jessica.

"All nice like that. Whine and cry, so I don't feel bad about not buying you the pearls."

"You don't have to feel bad," said Jessica.

"That's exactly what I mean," said Hank. "Don't act like that."

Jessica grinned. "Okay, then, buy me these pearls or I'll tell on you to another pirate captain."

"What are you talking about?" asked Hank.

"When pirates took over a big ship, any kind of ship, they'd ask the crew if the captain had been fair to them, and if the crew complained about their treatment, the pirates would torture the captain to death."

"That's more like it," said Hank. "Say nasty things like that."

"But I'd never really tell on you," said Jessica. "Because I love you. You're my brother."

"That's it," said Hank. "Give me the stupid pearls."

Jessica triumphantly swooped the pearls out of the treasure chest and handed them to Hank.

Hank put his doubloons on the checkout counter.

The clerk looked at the gold coins. He picked one up. Then he bit it.

"What are you doing?" asked Hank.

The clerk looked hard at Hank. "Where'd you get these?"

"From home," said Hank, which was true. He'd been at home when he'd eaten his cereal.

The clerk blinked. "I'm going to have to ask the manager about this." He took all four coins, went to the back of the store, and knocked on a door. Then he disappeared inside it for a minute. He came back quickly. "Did your parents say this was okay?"

Hank thought about that. His mom always allowed him to spend his own money any way he wanted. And these coins were his. "Yes."

"All right, then, it's a deal. Is there anything else you want? It looks like you're planning to be pirates in the parade, huh? You've got enough money here to get a toy pirate pistol, too, if you want." The clerk took a plastic pistol off the shelf behind him. "The black plastic looks pretty real, don't you think?"

Hank took the pistol and tucked it in his waistband. "Thanks."

"Is there enough money for me to get an earring?" Jessica asked, picking up a big gold hoop from the treasure chest.

"That earring costs a lot," said the clerk. Then he looked at the doubloons again. "But I guess you've got enough here."

Angel Talk

They're all decked out now," said the archangel. "They can spend the afternoon playing pirates."

"Except the parade starts soon."

"That's right. Hank will be in it on his bike, and Jessica will be left standing on the side."

The Little Angel of Fairness shook her head. "That would be terrible." She peeled the foil off a chocolate Kiss and put it in her mouth absentmindedly. "Somehow I've got to make sure that doesn't happen."

"How?"

"Well, the first thing is to make sure Hank realizes it shouldn't happen."

"Good start." The Archangel of Fairness smiled. "Can I have one of those Kisses?"

The little angel handed the archangel a Kiss.

They both stood sucking slowly, thinking.

The Parade

"You heard what the clerk said, Hank. You heard him." Jessica stood beside Hank and watched as he rubbed his bike with a cloth. "We should both be in the parade. As pirates. We can go in our schooner."

"That's what you've been planning all along, isn't it?" said Hank. "That's why you got out books about pirates."

Jessica smiled. "I wasn't exactly planning. I was just hoping."

Hank rubbed his handlebars. "Is that why you messed up my spaceship decals?"

"What? No," said Jessica. "I wouldn't hurt your bike."

"Then how do you explain that?" Hank pointed.

The decals were ragged at the edges, as

if someone had been trying to peel them off.

"Maybe the box rubbed against them," said Jessica doubtfully. "But they do look awful, Hank. You won't look good in the parade at all. It would be much better if we went together."

Hank looked at Jessica. It was true. Even if he put new spaceship decals on, his bike would look junky compared to how great they both would look in the schooner. "You'd have to put your hair under the bandanna so no one would know you're a girl. And you'd have to not tell anyone."

"Dead men tell no tales," said Jessica.

"What's that supposed to mean?"

"I don't know," said Jessica. "But pirates said it all the time."

"Pirates were weird," said Hank.

"Not all of them. Some were just ordinary fishermen or sailors who got ambushed by pirates and joined them. President Fillmore's great-grandfather was a pirate like that," said Jessica.

"Who was President Fillmore?" asked Hank.

"I don't know. Some president or other. The point is," said Jessica, "I won't tell anyone. I swear, Hank."

"Okay."

"Yay!" Jessica threw her arms around Hank.

"Don't kiss me. Just help me get this schooner back together and let's go."

Angel Talk

"You scraped his decals," said the archangel.

"That's not like pushing a box in front of his bike," said the little angel.

"But it *is* bad. You ruined his property."

"He still has a few left. I checked in his drawer," said the little angel.

"That doesn't justify ruining the ones on his bike," said the archangel. "You know, you can't just go forcing people to do things your way by not giving them a choice."

"Hank needed to be forced."

"How do you know? Maybe he would have come around on his own. Or maybe," said the archangel, "just maybe he would have had a better idea of his own. You never know what people will think of if they're left to their own resources."

The Little Angel of Fairness didn't like this conversation. It reminded her of her friend, the Little Angel of Friendship, and how he'd said that she always chose the games they played and he was forced to go along. "Hank's happy about going in the schooner with Jessica," she said softly. "You can tell. He is making progress."

"Yes, I think he is," said the archangel. "But I'll try not to force him anymore."

Hair

Main Street in front of the library was already crowded with people. There were fire trucks and the high school band and the long line of floats. And in the middle of it all were about fifty boys on bikes, most of them dressed in pirate outfits.

"We look better than any of them," said Jessica to Hank.

"Hush. And keep that patch over your eye so no one recognizes you." Hank kept his eyes down, hoping none of his friends would ask him who his partner was on the schooner.

"Great-looking costumes," came a loud voice.

Hank looked up into the face of a high school kid.

"You two are almost like a small float. Why

don't you go to the front of the bikes?"

"Yay!" said Jessica.

Hank looked around. The boys on the bikes closest to them were all watching. "Be quiet," he whispered to Jessica. "We can't go fast," he said to the high school kid. "We have to walk our bikes."

"That's okay. The parade is slow. Get on up there." The kid led them to their new spot.

The drummers gave out a low roll, and the parade started. They went up Main Street to the town hall, then left onto Park Avenue. People lined both sides of the parade path. They waved and pointed. Lots of people pointed at Hank and Jessica.

Jessica laughed. "Oh, I love this, Hank," she shouted over the noise of the band. "This is so much fun. Oh, thank you, Hank."

"You're like a real girl pirate," said Hank. "Like that Anne pirate."

"I don't want to be like Anne. I want to be like Mary. She was a lot nicer. And she was more interesting, too. When they caught Mary, she didn't apologize. She just talked and talked about what a great life pirates had."

"She was nuts," yelled Hank. "Did they hang her?"

"No. But they hanged all the men pirates they caught."

"That's not fair," said Hank.

"You're right."

Hank looked at Jessica. There she was, a pirate just as good as any boy pirate. He pulled her bandanna off.

"What are you doing?"

"Now they know you're a girl," said Hank. "And they should. You're a great pirate, Jessica."

"Thanks. So are you."

Little Angels at Play

"ow'd it go?" asked the Little Angel of Friendship.

"Good," said the Little Angel of Fairness.

"All right, then. Let's play the game you were talking about. The one with gold coins."

"Sure, that's a great game." The Little Angel of Fairness reached into her pocket for the coins. Then she stopped. "Didn't you have a game in mind?"

"It doesn't matter. You're right: Your games are always the best."

"Did I say that? What a jerk I was. I want to play your game," said the Little Angel of Fairness.

"Really?"

"Really. We can play the coin game another time."

"Okay." The Little Angel of Friendship gave a shy smile. "It's not really anything special. I didn't make it up. It's just horseshoes." He opened a cloth bag and took out a post and six horseshoes. He set the post up. "We have to stand back pretty far. Here." The Little Angel of Friendship handed the Little Angel of Fairness three horseshoes. "You throw first."

"Thanks." The Little Angel of Fairness tossed her horseshoe. It flipped over and over and landed with a sharp *ring* right against the post.

"That sounded like a bell to me," said the Little Angel of Friendship. His eyes sparkled, and he lifted an eyebrow.

The newest Archangel of Fairness laughed. "And isn't it the best sound you've ever heard?" She spread her newly earned wings and flew around her friend.

Jessica's costume

You can dress like a pirate, too. Use your imagination, and make a pirate costume like Jessica's. What did Jessica use to put together her costume?

- an old striped shirt
- black pants
- a bandanna or kerchief
- a piece of black fabric for an eye patch

What can you find around your house for a pirate costume?

Don't miss these other
Aladdin *Angelwings* stories:

№. 7

April Flowers

№. 8

Playing Games

№. 9

Lies and Lemons